Level 2   Book 3

words

stories

CW00840460

The Enormous Turnip

Stories adapted by Shirley Jackson
Illustrated by Rebecca Harry
Series designed by Jeannette Slater

Copyright © 1999 Egmont World Limited.
All rights reserved.
Published in Great Britain by Egmont World Limited,
Deanway Technology Centre, Wilmslow Road,
Handforth, Cheshire SK9 3FB
Printed in Germany
ISBN 0 7498 4361 6

enormous

turnip

Once upon a time,
an old man planted
some turnip seeds.

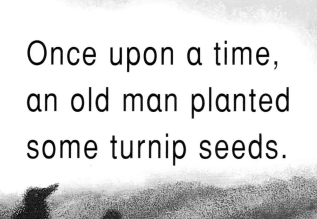

new word **planted**

The turnip seeds grew.
The turnip seeds grew
and grew. The turnip
seeds grew and grew
and grew.

New word **grew**

"I want to pull up the enormous turnip," said the old man.

ew words **want pull**

The old man pulled
and pulled. But he
could not pull up the
enormous turnip.

new words **pulled** **could**

An old woman came.

"I want to pull up that enormous turnip," said the old man.

o new words

"I will help you," said the old woman.

new words

The old man and the old woman pulled and pulled.

But they could not pull up the enormous turnip.

o new words

A boy came.

"We want to pull up that enormous turnip," said the old woman.

"I will help you," said the boy

o new words

The old man and the old woman and the boy pulled and pulled.

But they could not pull up the enormous turnip.

o new words

A girl came.

"We want to pull up
that enormous turnip,"
said the boy.

"I will help you," said
the girl.

The old man and the old woman and the boy and the girl pulled and pulled.

UP came the enormous turnip.

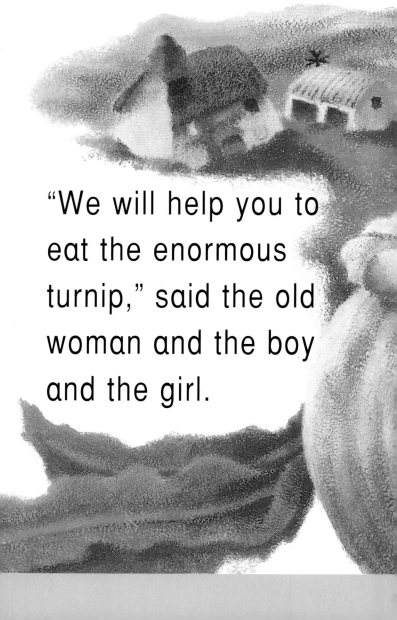

"We will help you to eat the enormous turnip," said the old woman and the boy and the girl.

And they did!